MR LEON'S PARIS

Barroux

PHOENIX YARD
BOOKS

To Sempé

Translated by Sarah Ardizzone

Hello, I'm **Mr Leon** and I drive a taxi.
I've been criss-crossing this city day and night;
when I started out
there was only one channel
and the telly was still in black and white.

Now, everybody knows me by name.
It's "Hey, Mr Leon!" here and "Hey, Mr Leon!" there.
I've clocked up some miles behind this wheel.

And strange folks too, I've seen a few
in thirty years on the job – some unusual customers.
"Hell's Passage please, Mr Leon, and step on it."
"Chill out, my friend, and don't singe my seats!"

I've never left my city, but I've seen a thing or two,
I've even glimpsed countries on the other side of the world.
"7, Pyramid Street, via Cairo Place please, Mr Leon."
"Hop in, off we go!"

Night and day, whatever the weather,
I keep my meter ticking over.
On **Bad Boys' Road**,
Great Gangster Street,
Groggy Square...
I've never had a spot of bother.

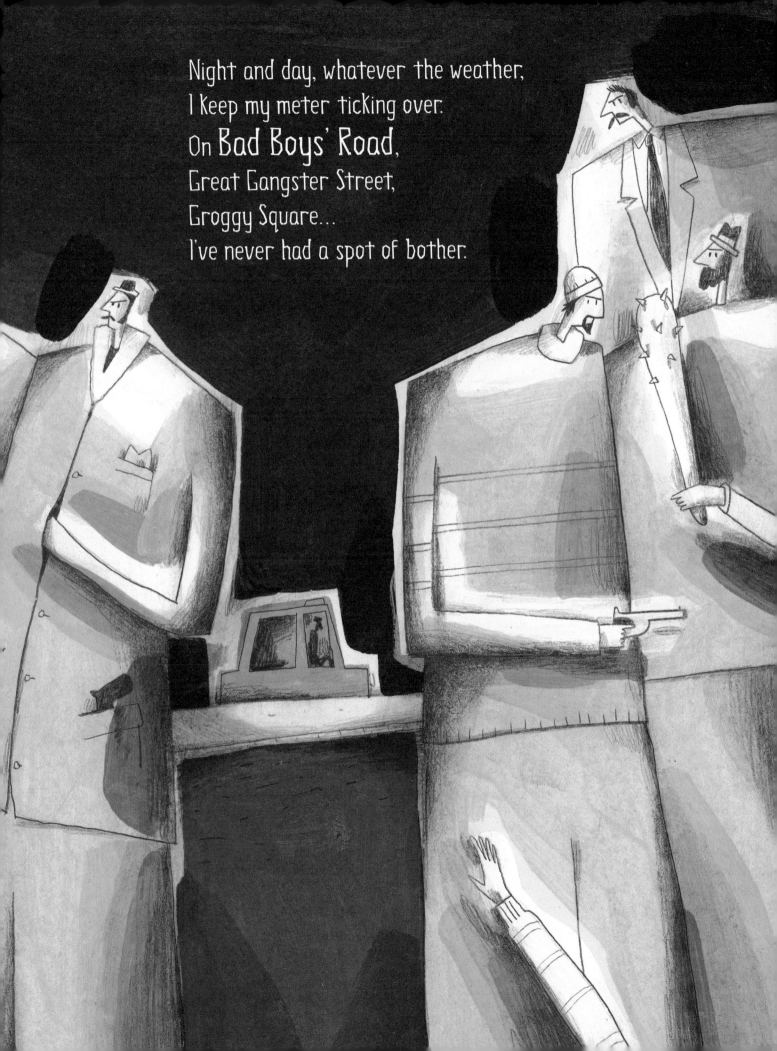

I've heard some gossip in my time
about life and love.
    People like to let their secrets out of the bag.
    "Peking Passage with a stop-off
    on China Street, please Mr Leon."
    "Hop in, you pair of lovebirds, off we go!"

"Let's check I've got this one right?
Going to **9 Hen Road** from Chicken Street,
with a pick-up on Cockerel Avenue,
steering clear of Fox Boulevard.
That won't be easy, but I'll do my best.
Hop in everybody, let's hit the road!"

Passengers talk about everything and nothing,
about the rain, or the nice weather we're having.
But I'm always snug inside my yellow car.
"7, North Pole Street, just by Canada Road.
Drive carefully please, Mr Leon."
"Hop in, off we go!"

Stuck in traffic jams, I often daydream...
The noise of the engines like beating dreams,
the buildings like baobab trees...
In my head I redraw the city.
"Morning, Mr Leon, left on Congo Road please,
all the way to Senegal Street."

"Hop in, off we go!"

Every Monday, I pick up Mr Slimane
from outside his apartment block,
and every Monday – for ten years now –
he grins and greets me: "Salam alaikum,
Mr Leon my friend, 10 Morocco Street,
11 Tunisia Avenue, 12 Algeria Boulevard."
"Hop in, Mr Slimane, off we go!"

On Tuesdays, I pick up Henri the handyman from Hammer Yard.
On Wednesdays, it's Jeanette the hairdresser from Scissor Row.
On Thursdays, I head to Englishman's Street for Captain Scott.

And on Fridays? Ah, Fridays,
it's pretty Suzie from **Princess Court**, of course.

I've never had a single accident,
not a bump or a scratch on my cab.
I stop at the lights, check my indicators.
"16, Paradise Street, please."
"You're my last ever passengers,
so hop in, off we go!"

Tomorrow...

...I'm stopping, I'm hanging up my hat.

Driver in search of new adventures
offers taxi for sale:
handsome cab, canary yellow,
high mileage but fit to go.

"Hey, Taxi!
Straight to the harbour!"

I'm off on the waves to discover the world,
to walk for hours along Liberty Street.

And even drift up Moon Street
if the wind is good...

Mr Leon's Paris

Hardback ISBN: 978-1-907912-07-8
Paperback ISBN: 978-1-907912-08-5

First published in French in 2011 under the title *Le Paris de Léon*
by Actes Sud, Arles, France.
This edition published in Great Britain by Phoenix Yard Books, 2012.

Phoenix Yard Books Ltd
Phoenix Yard
65 King's Cross Road
London
WC1X 9LW
www.phoenixyardbooks.com

1 3 5 7 9 10 8 6 4 2

A CIP catalogue record for this book is available from the British Library
Printed in Singapore